This Topsy and Tim book belongs to

Published by Ladybird Books Ltd
80 Strand London WC2R ORL
A Penguin Company

009-12 11 10 9

ISBN-13: 978-1-84422-582-8

Printed in China

Help a Friend

Jean and **Gareth Adamson**

One morning Topsy and Tim met
Stevie Dunton at the school gate.
Stevie looked upset.
"What's wrong, Stevie?" asked Tim.
"I hate school," said Stevie.

Stevie cheered up when they went into the classroom, but at break he didn't want to go out to play.

"What's wrong, Stevie?" asked Miss Terry.

"Nothing," said Stevie, and he went out.

Topsy and Tim were playing 'It' in
the playground with their friends.
"Come on, Stevie. Kerry's It,"
called Topsy.
Stevie joined in and Kerry began to
chase him.

Stevie was a good runner. He was getting away from Kerry when James, the biggest boy in the class, stuck out his foot and tripped Stevie up.

Stevie began to cry.
"Cry baby, cry baby!" shouted James
and his friend Sylvie. Some of the
children laughed. Topsy and Tim didn't,
but they didn't know what to do.

After break it was P.E. The children had to change into their plimsolls. Soon everyone was ready except Stevie.
"Come on, Stevie, we're all waiting for you," said Miss Terry.
"I can't find one of my plimsolls," said Stevie.

Miss Terry was cross and made
everyone look for it.
"There it is, Stevie, hanging on your
peg," said Topsy.
"How did it get there?" said Stevie.
Tim saw Sylvie wink at James.

After school Topsy and Tim told
Mummy about James and Sylvie.
"James keeps on being nasty to Stevie,"
said Topsy.
"And Sylvie copies him," said Tim.
"I think James is a bit of a bully," said
Mummy. "And Sylvie is, too."

"What's a bully?" asked Topsy.
"Someone who likes to hurt or frighten other people," said Mummy. "And bullies make everyone too afraid to tell a grown-up."
"I'm not afraid," said Tim.
"I am!" said Topsy.
"Well, I am a bit," said Tim.

"It was brave of you to tell me," said
Mummy. "You should tell Miss Terry, too."
"That's telling tales," said Topsy.
"That's what bullies want you to think,"
said Mummy. "That's how they get away
with hurting other people."

The next day at school, Tim told Stevie
what Mummy had said about bullies.
"Have you told your mum about
James?" asked Topsy.
"No," said Stevie, "I don't want her to
think I'm telling tales."

As Stevie was hanging up his anorak,
James ran in. He grabbed Stevie's
schoolbag and threw it across
the cloakroom.
"Catch, Sylvie," he shouted.

Sylvie ran to catch it.
"That's not yours!" shouted Topsy.
"Give it back to Stevie," yelled Tim.
Sylvie grabbed the bag and threw it back
to James.

James dropped the bag on the floor and everything fell out. Everyone laughed, except Topsy and Tim and Stevie. Suddenly Miss Terry came in.
"What is going on?" she said. "Stevie, what a mess!" Stevie began to cry.

"James did it, Miss Terry," said Topsy.
"He always does nasty things to Stevie."
"He's a bully," said Tim.
"All right children, calm down," said Miss
Terry. "It's time I had a talk with the
whole class."

When all the children were settled in the classroom, Miss Terry talked to them about bullying. Then she asked them to tell her what bullies did.

"They hit you and hurt you," said Andy Anderson.
"They call you names," said Rai.
"They leave you out of the game," said Louise.
"They make your friends be nasty to you," said Alice.

"Why are bullies so unkind?"
asked Topsy.
"Sometimes bullies have been bullied
themselves," said Miss Terry. "Then they
take it out on someone else because it
makes them feel big."
Topsy and Tim began to feel a little bit
sorry for the bullies.

"I hate bullying!" said Kerry.
"Does anyone here like bullying?"
asked Miss Terry.
"NO!" shouted all the children.

After school Topsy and Tim ran down
to the school gates with Stevie, to
meet their mums.
"Was school all right today?" asked
Stevie's mum.
"Yes it was," said Stevie. "I've got
something to tell you."

Stevie told his mum that James had been bullying him.

"Oh dear!" said Stevie's mum, looking upset.

"Don't worry mum," said Stevie. "Topsy and Tim told Miss Terry all about it and I feel much happier now."

Stevie's mum gave him a big hug.

"Goodbye, Stevie," said Topsy and Tim.
Stevie smiled and waved at them.
"See you tomorrow," he called.